First published in Great Britain 2019
This edition published in Great Britain 2024 by Farshore
An imprint of HarperCollins*Publishers*, 1 London Bridge Street, London, SE1 9GF
www.farshore.co.uk

HarperCollins*Publishers*
Macken House, 39/40 Mayor Street Upper,
Dublin 1, D01 C9W8, Ireland

Written by Frankie Jones
Additional illustrations by Emily McGorman-Bruce and Nigel Parkinson

BEANO.COM

A Beano Studios Product © DC Thomson & Co Ltd. (2024)

ISBN 978 0 00 861538 3
Printed in Great Britain
001

Stay safe online. Any website addresses listed in this book are correct at the
time of going to print. However, Farshore is not responsible for content hosted by
third parties. Please be aware that online content can be subject to change and
websites can contain content that is unsuitable for children. We advise that all
children are supervised when using the internet.

MIX
Paper | Supporting
responsible forestry
FSC™ C007454

This book contains FSC™ certified paper and other controlled
sources to ensure responsible forest management.

For more information visit: www.harpercollins.co.uk/green

BEANO

HOW TO DRAW

CONTENTS

Why I Love Comics

Drawing comics is fun! There, the secret is out! It can be long hours and hard work, but it's fun!

I started drawing when I was under two years old. And I've never stopped. If it wasn't fun, would I do that?

Telling a story in pictures isn't the same as telling a story just in words. The pictures should tell the story in a clear, funny and exciting way, and the words should add detail, giving extra depth and humour.

There aren't very many rules in making comics. Action should always come from the left, and you read a strip from the left and then down the page. Otherwise, anything goes!

Nigel Parkinson
Illustrator of Dennis & Gnasher Unleashed, plus the Beano Boomics and more!

Drawing Dennis and Gnasher is great. They only do things that are heroic, wild, funny, extreme or exciting. So when they run, it's wild or exciting. When they stand still, it's heroic. When they're sad, it's extreme.

When you create your own comic, your characters can say anything you want, go anywhere, do anything. There are lots of ideas and tips in this book, but feel free to experiment and make up your own characters and stories! Whatever you choose to do, make it heroic, exciting and extreme. And above all, have fun!

WHY I LOVE COMICS

MY LOVE OF BOOKS STARTED BEFORE I COULD EVEN READ. AFTER DISCOVERING PICTURE BOOKS, IT WASN'T LONG BEFORE I MADE THE MOVE INTO COMICS. I GREW UP READING GARFIELD, ORSON'S FARM AND OF COURSE BEANO AND DANDY! THAT'S WHEN MY LOVE OF COMICS BEGAN AND IT'S SOMETHING I'VE NEVER GROWN OUT OF!

I HAD ALWAYS LOVED DRAWING, AND READING COMICS INSPIRED ME TO MAKE MY OWN. I WOULD DREAM UP ADVENTURES FOR MY FAVOURITE CHARACTERS FROM BOOKS, TV SHOWS OR COMICS AND FILL SKETCH BOOKS WITH LITTLE SKITS!

IT'S GREAT FUN TO THINK OF YOUR OWN STORIES FOR YOUR FAVOURITE CHARACTERS, AND EVERYONE SHOULD BE ENCOURAGED TO TRY MAKING COMICS THEMSELVES – THIS BOOK IS THE PERFECT PLACE TO START.

FOLLOW THE STEP-BY-STEPS TO LEARN HOW TO DRAW DENNIS, MINNIE, GNASHER, JEM AND ROGER, AND HAVE A LOOK AT THE STORY IDEAS TO HELP YOU CREATE YOUR VERY OWN ADVENTURES.

WHEN YOU READ A BOOK, PEOPLE HAVE THEIR OWN INTERPRETATIONS OF HOW THE SCENES LOOK. WITH A COMIC, YOU CAN CONVEY EXACTLY WHAT YOU WANT PEOPLE TO SEE, SO THEY ARE SHARING IN YOUR IMAGINATION! WHAT COULD BE BETTER THAN THAT?

EMILY MCGORMAN-BRUCE BEANO STUDIOS ILLUSTRATOR OF BEANO BOSS, HAR HAR'S JOKE SHOP AND HARSHA'S PRANK ACADEMY.

HOW TO USE THIS BOOK

Is a weekly Beano comic not enough for you? Do you have loads of stories just begging to be told? Well, why not create a Beano comic of your own?

Beano has been around for over 85(!) years, and in that time, there have been LOADS of illustrators, comic book artists and writers coming up with stories for Beano. If they can do it, why can't you?

This book is filled with everything you need to learn to be able to create your very own Beano comic book, from coming up with a blamazing story to how to draw your favourite characters, then putting it all together in a comic book.

There's space throughout to practise on the page, but be sure not to draw in this book if it doesn't belong to you – it's not worth falling out with any friends or librarians over!

So, what are you waiting for? Sharpen your pencil and let's get creative!

Things You'll Need

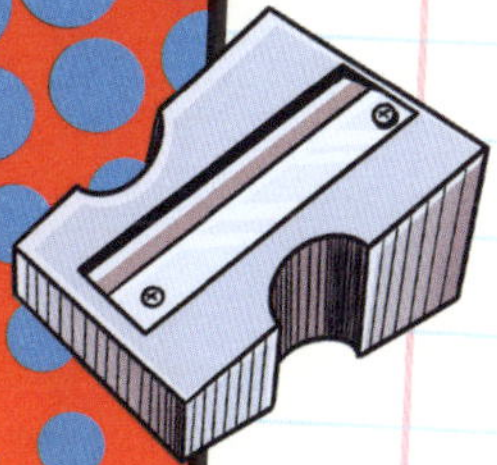

Pencils

A pencil sharpener

An eraser

Felt tip pens
(It's useful to have black pens
in a range of thicknesses)

Spare paper or a sketchbook

Beano comics (Not essential,
but could come in handy!)

A 6-sided dice

WHAT IS A COMIC?

If you want to know what a comic is, ~~have you been living under a rock?~~ you're in the right place!

A comic is a (usually funny) story told through a series of panels, which contain drawings and words. A comic strip is the sequence of drawings that tells the story, and these often appear in collections within comic books.

Beano is one of the most famous comic books for kids, and has been going for over 85 years. Some of the most recognisable comic book characters come from Beano, including Dennis Menace, Minnie Makepeace, Bananaman, Billy Whizz and original cover star Big Eggo.

A COMIC STRIP IS MADE UP OF PANELS . . .

THE STORY IS TOLD IN A FEW WAYS . . .

A SPEECH BALLOON SHOWS DIALOGUE.

YOU JUST READ MY MIND. THOUGHT BUBBLES SHOW WHAT CHARACTERS ARE THINKING.

CAPTION BOXES MOVE THE STORY ALONG.

PICTURES SPEAK A THOUSAND WORDS. MOST OF THE ACTION IS SHOWN IN THE DRAWINGS!

SOMETIMES THE EDITOR ADDS CAPTIONS TOO! - THE ED

It takes a whole team of people to make a comic like Beano.

A WRITER COMES UP WITH THE STORYLINES FOR THE COMIC AND PLANS WHAT WILL HAPPEN IN EACH PANEL OF THE STRIP.

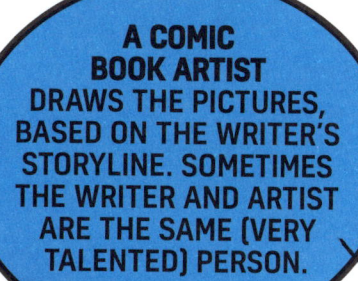

A COMIC BOOK ARTIST DRAWS THE PICTURES, BASED ON THE WRITER'S STORYLINE. SOMETIMES THE WRITER AND ARTIST ARE THE SAME (VERY TALENTED) PERSON.

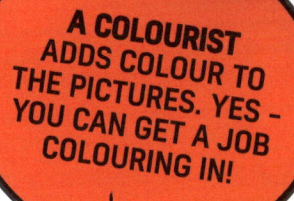

A COLOURIST ADDS COLOUR TO THE PICTURES. YES – YOU CAN GET A JOB COLOURING IN!

AN EDITOR MAKES SURE EVERYTHING MAKES SENSE AND PUTS THE COMIC BOOK TOGETHER. SOMETIMES THE EDITOR WILL CHIP IN TO THE COMIC STRIP WITH THEIR OWN IDEAS!

But this book puts you in charge. You are the writer, artist, colourist and editor – all rolled into one!

PENCIL, INK AND COLOUR

All comic artists work in different ways, using a range of materials and tools. Whatever their method, they all agree on one thing: you've got to do things in the right order to make sure your finished drawing has no mistakes and doesn't get smudged!

Here's the best way to plan, outline and finish your drawing:

PENCIL – Plan your drawing in pencil. You can add in guidelines, erase any mistakes and make sure the drawing is perfect before you add ink or felt tip. Make sure to use a light line, so you can erase any marks after inking.

INK – Draw the outline and details of your character in black. We recommend using a black felt tip or fineliner pen.

BLACK – Using your black felt tips, colour in any black details, such as the stripes on Dennis's jumper.

DRY – Let your black ink fully dry, to avoid it from running into your colours and smudging.

COLOUR – Add one colour at a time, making sure to colour in as neatly as possible! Let each colour dry before adding the next.

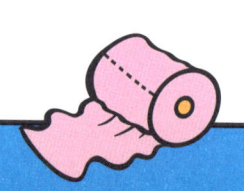

Dennis has been drawn here in a very light pencil.
Use a black pen to draw the outlines and
fill in the black areas, then colour him in!

COME UP WITH A STORY

Comics may be told with images in panels, but at their core, they are still stories. Without a story, a comic is just a drawing, after all. So before we even take a look at drawing, let's first figure out the tale you'd like to tell.

There are many ways to come up with stories: you can either take scenes from your own life or come up with something entirely original – or a bit of both!

Use this chapter to help inspire ideas and structure your stories, so that when you come to draw your comics, you are already armed with a hilarious tale to tell.

STORY STARTERS

Every great comic starts with a story. But first you need an idea! A good way to come up with a story idea is to think of a 'what if' scenario. Here are some Beanotown what ifs to inspire you!

ROLL A STORY

Still stuck for ideas?
Just grab a dice and get inspired!
Roll the dice once for each category to come
up with a Beano-riffic storyline. You must include
everything you rolled in your new comic strip!

ROLL 1

CHOOSE A MAIN CHARACTER

1: DENNIS
2: MINNIE
3: JEM
4: ROGER
5: WALTER
6: RUBI

ROLL 2

CHOOSE A SECOND CHARACTER

1: GNASHER
2: HARSHA
3: BANANAMAN
4: CALAMITY JAMES
5: SKETCH KHAD
6: BILLY WHIZZ

ROLL 3

CHOOSE A LOCATION

1: BASH STREET SCHOOL
2: HORRIBLE HALL
3: BEANOTOWN MUSEUM
4: DUCK ISLAND
5: YOUR HOUSE
6: THE MOON

ROLL 4

CHOOSE AN EVENT

1: A BIRTHDAY PARTY
2: FIRST DAY OF SCHOOL
3: SKATEBOARDING
COMPETITION
4: SCHOOL TRIP
5: LAST DAY OF SCHOOL
6: DENTIST APPOINTMENT

WRITE WHAT YOU ROLLED HERE, AND THEN FILL IN A BLANK STORY SHEET WITH YOUR IDEAS! YOU CAN COME BACK TO THIS PAGE – THE COMBINATIONS ARE ALMOST* UNLIMITED!

MAIN CHARACTER
SECOND CHARACTER
LOCATION
EVENT
OBJECT
WORD

ROLL 5

CHOOSE AN OBJECT

1: STINK BOMB
2: SLINGSHOT
3: SAUSAGES
4: WHOOPEE CUSHION
5: FOOTBALL
6: SKATEBOARD

MAIN CHARACTER
SECOND CHARACTER
LOCATION
EVENT
OBJECT
WORD

ROLL 6

CHOOSE A WORD

1: DISASTER
2: MAGICAL
3: MYSTERY
4: PRANK
5: ALIEN
6: COMPETITION

MAIN CHARACTER
SECOND CHARACTER
LOCATION
EVENT
OBJECT
WORD

*ACTUALLY, THERE ARE 46,656 POSSIBLE COMBINATIONS – THAT'S A LOT OF COMIC STRIPS TO WRITE!

MAIN CHARACTER
SECOND CHARACTER
LOCATION
EVENT
OBJECT
WORD

THE COMIC CHALLENGE

Don't have a dice to roll a story? Never fear! The Beano Comic Challenge is here! Plan a quick comic including the following characters, locations, objects and words. Draw your comic in the empty panels below!

 RUBI

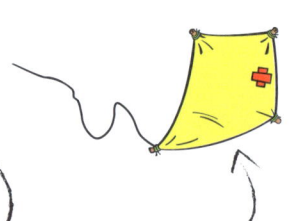

SCIENTIFIC FACT

WHO?
MAKE SURE THIS BEANO STAR IS IN THE COMIC.

WHERE?
HERE'S WHERE TO DRAW YOUR CHARACTER.

WHAT?
SEE IF YOU CAN SNEAK THIS INTO YOUR STORY.

WORDS?
SLIP THESE WORDS INTO YOUR SPEECH BALLOONS.

Did you enjoy that challenge? Then why not try out another, using the new prompts below? If you're not ready to draw yet, simply write down your plot points in the boxes below.

BERTIE

CLASS 3C

MEGA STINK BOMB

PRANK DISASTER

WHO?
MAKE SURE THIS BEANO STAR IS IN THE COMIC.

WHERE?
HERE'S WHERE TO DRAW YOUR CHARACTER.

WHAT?
SEE IF YOU CAN SNEAK THIS INTO YOUR STORY.

WORDS?
SLIP THESE WORDS INTO YOUR SPEECH BALLOONS.

CREATING STORIES

Now that you've got an idea, it's time to shape it into a blamazing story for your comic!

All stories have a BEGINNING, MIDDLE and END. This is called your plot. What happens at each point is up to you. Below are some pointers on each section.

At the BEGINNING of your story, you should introduce the main character and set the scene. Once you've done that, it's time to bring in a problem for your character to solve.

The MIDDLE of the story is where the action happens – your character must tackle the problem you've given them, and something will usually go wrong.

The END of the story should wrap everything up to a satisfying close. The problem should be fixed – and you can decide whether the story has a happy or sad ending.

DONT FORGET TO HAVE FUN AND MAKE YOUR STORY AS BANANAS AS YOU WANT - JUST LIKE ME!

STORY SHEET

Try filling in this story sheet, to help you plan what happens in your strip. There are more of these at the back of the book, so you can plan even more stories!

> SOMETIMES IT'S EASIER TO COME UP WITH A TITLE **AFTER** YOU'VE WORKED OUT THE PLOT.

TITLE

....

BEGINNING

WHO IS THE MAIN CHARACTER OF THE STORY? ....

WHAT DOES THE CHARACTER WANT OR NEED? ....

....

WHERE IS THE STORY SET? ....

MIDDLE

WHAT PROBLEM DOES YOUR CHARACTER COME UP AGAINST?

....

....

> WORKING OUT WHAT YOUR CHARACTER **WANTS** OR **NEEDS** IS A GOOD WAY TO FIND A PROBLEM FOR THE MIDDLE. PERHAPS THEY CAN'T GET WHAT THEY WANT.

HOW DOES YOUR CHARACTER REACT TO THE PROBLEM? ....

....

HOW DOES THE CHARACTER FEEL? ....

WHAT'S THE MAIN ACTION? ....

....

END

> YOU CAN ALWAYS LEAVE YOUR STORY ON A CLIFFHANGER AND CONTINUE IT IN ANOTHER STRIP!

HOW IS THE PROBLEM SOLVED? ....

....

HOW DOES YOUR CHARACTER FEEL? ....

....

STORY SHEET

IDEA!

TITLE

A Skate of Emergency

BEGINNING

WHO IS THE MAIN CHARACTER OF THE STORY? Dennis Menace

WHAT DOES THE CHARACTER WANT OR NEED? To win Beanotown's annual skateboarding championship

WHERE IS THE STORY SET? Beanotown skatepark

MIDDLE

WHAT PROBLEM DOES YOUR CHARACTER COME UP AGAINST? Aliens have invaded Beanotown and are threatening to wipe out the skatepark

HOW DOES YOUR CHARACTER REACT TO THE PROBLEM? Decides to take on the aliens in a fight for Beanotown's freedom

HOW DOES THE CHARACTER FEEL? Scared but determined

WHAT'S THE MAIN ACTION? A huge prank to scare off the aliens

END

HOW IS THE PROBLEM SOLVED? They weren't aliens at all, just Wilbur and Walter dressed up as them in a ploy to shut down the skatepark

HOW DOES YOUR CHARACTER FEEL? Mega happy when not only do they save the skatepark, but Dennis also wins his skating competition!

STORY SHEET

GOT ANOTHER IDEA? COME UP WITH ANOTHER PLOT HERE!

TITLE

BEGINNING

WHO IS THE MAIN CHARACTER OF THE STORY?

WHAT DOES THE CHARACTER WANT OR NEED?

WHERE IS THE STORY SET?

MIDDLE

WHAT PROBLEM DOES YOUR CHARACTER COME UP AGAINST?

HOW DOES YOUR CHARACTER REACT TO THE PROBLEM?

HOW DOES THE CHARACTER FEEL?

WHAT'S THE MAIN ACTION?

END

HOW IS THE PROBLEM SOLVED?

THERE ARE MORE OF THESE PAGES AT THE BACK OF THE BOOK FOR YOU TO FILL IN!

HOW DOES YOUR CHARACTER FEEL?

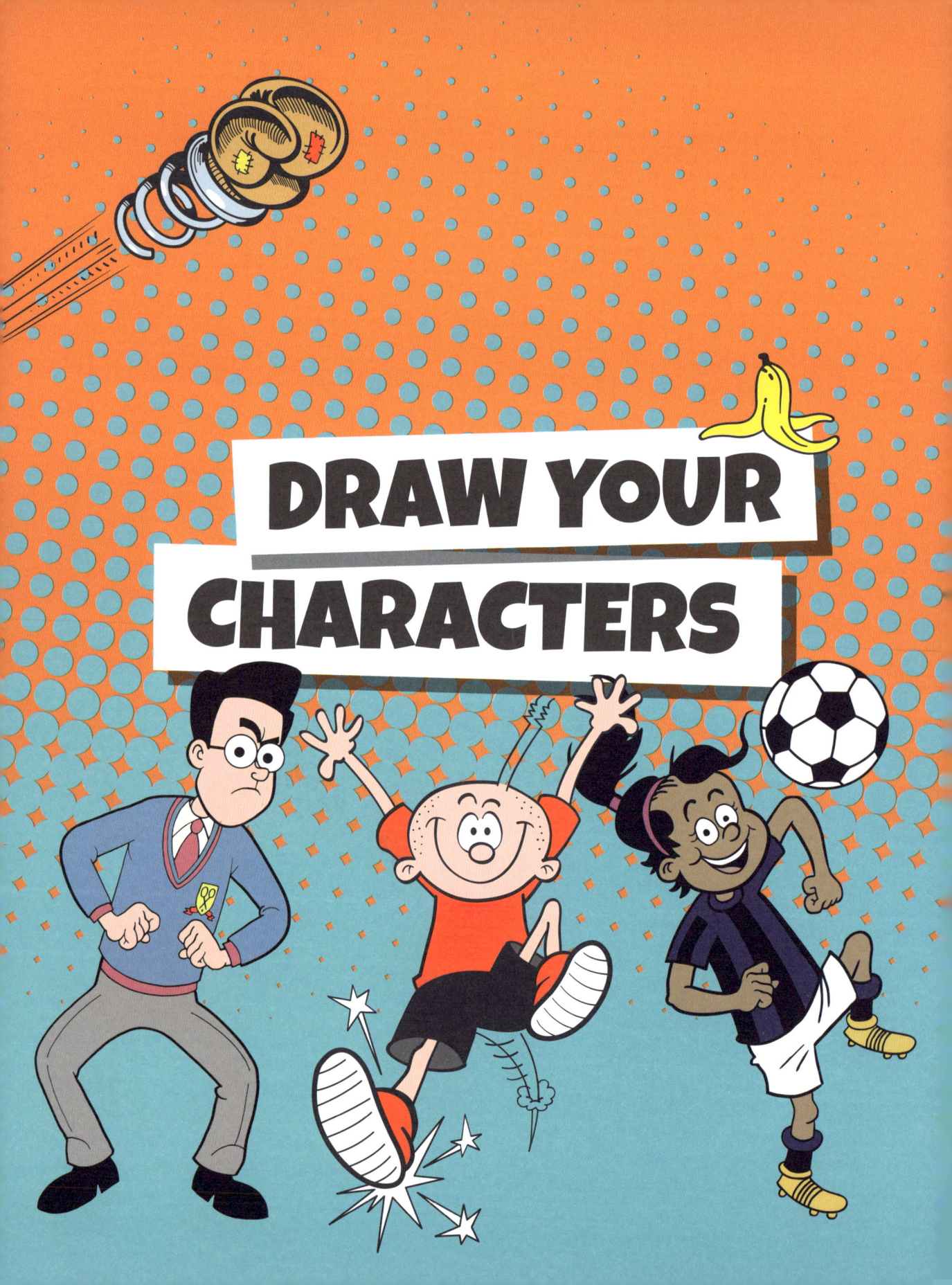

Before you can create a comic, you first need to be able to draw your characters! When illustrating your awesome stories, you'll need to draw your characters in all kinds of dynamic positions, with different facial expressions.

Use the following pages to practise drawing the various Beano characters in their many poses, learning as you go, so that you can draw them in your stories. Thankfully, there are plenty of characters for you to practise with, so you'll soon be a pro!

Either draw on the page or – if this book doesn't belong to you – use a piece of paper or a sketchbook.

HOW TO DRAW DENNIS

Nigel illustrates Dennis every week! Follow the step–by–steps below to draw Beano's iconic character.

1

Dennis is a bold, heroic sort of fellow, so start by drawing a confident line from top to toe. Sketch in a few quick lines for where his head, shoulders and waist will be.

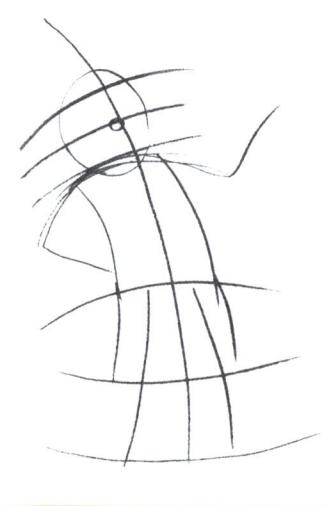

2

On the centre line, where the head is, draw in the nose. Everything is easier to fit in if you've decided where the nose will be. Add in a rough line for the arms and legs.

3

Start to fill in the shapes for the arms, hands, torso, legs and feet. Sketch in where the eyes will go.

EXPERT TIP

DENNIS IS ALWAYS DYNAMIC. HE'S ALWAYS ON THE MOVE, LEANING IN OR LEANING BACK. MAKE SURE HIS POSTURE REFLECTS THIS!

4

Add a bit more detail to Dennis's body and, most importantly, decide on the expression he is pulling!

5

Fill in details like ears, stripes, socks and finally hair – go wild and enjoy adding that hair!

6

Rub out the construction lines and there's Dennis! You just need to add colour to finish him off.

NOT BAD!

DENNIS'S
POSES AND EXPRESSIONS

Dennis gets up to plenty of mischief, so you'll need to be able to draw him in different poses and pulling different faces. Here are some ideas for you to use in your comic strips! Practise drawing your favourite poses and expressions on a spare sheet of paper.

Practise drawing Dennis by adding him to this comic strip.
Fill in the speech balloons with hilarious dialogue.

EXPERT TIP

PLAN YOUR STRIP ON A PIECE OF PAPER BEFORE DRAWING IT IN HERE. REMEMBER TO USE A PENCIL FIRST!

HOW TO DRAW GNASHER

1

Gnasher is Dennis's faithful sidekick, and is never far from his friend. Check out Nigel's step-by-step instructions for drawing this Abyssinian wire-haired tripe hound.

2

Start by drawing your guideline. Just like Dennis, Gnasher is always on the move, so curve the line backwards. Add in some rough lines to show where the eyes, head and legs will go.

3

Add in circles for the head and body, as well as four lines for the arms and legs.

Start to fill in some rough shapes: Gnasher's upturned snout, his ears, eyes, arms and legs.

GNASH GNASH!

4

Add some more details such as Gnasher's toothy grin and his paws.

5

Fur is the last thing to add – go wild!

6

Rub out the construction lines and then add colour!

EXPERT TIP

GNASHER IS THE DOG VERSION OF DENNIS: STURDY, BRAVE AND ALWAYS CHEERFUL. TRY TO REFLECT THIS IN YOUR DRAWINGS.

GNASHER'S POSES AND EXPRESSIONS

Here are some Gnasher poses and expressions for you to copy.

Practise drawing Gnasher by adding him to this comic strip and filling in the speech and thought bubbles.

35

HOW TO DRAW MINNIE

Minnie is always getting up to mischief and is a great character to draw! Follow Emily's step-by-step instructions and try your hand at drawing this MissChief!

1

Rough out a pose with some basic shapes - press lightly here as you'll want to rub out these lines later. Put a cross on the face to show the direction she's going to be looking.

2

Using your rough sketch as a base, draw the shape of her face - placing her nose in the middle. Draw in her beret, pigtails, hands and add the cuffs of her clothes.

3

Add detail to the hair, leaving a few bits out of place at the bottom and add ribbons. Draw in her clothes and don't forget the pom-pom on her beret!

EXPERT TIP

MINNIE IS MISCHIEVOUS - MAKE SURE SHE HAS A GOOD GRIN!

4

Draw in Minnie's hands using the guidelines you made earlier and don't forget her shoes. Now is a good time to draw her legs too – including those knobbly knees!

5

It's time for the face. Draw the eyes touching the circle you made for the nose. Add in a big smile to show she's up to something! Draw in the stripes on her jumper too.

6

Make the smile into a toothy grin. Now she really looks like she's up to something! Go over everything in pen and colour in the black areas.

7

Erase your pencil lines underneath the pen (make sure the pen is dry first) and now you're ready to add colour!

GASSY FIZZ

MINNIE'S
POSES AND EXPRESSIONS

Copy and use these Minnie poses in your next mincredible comic.

Add Minnie into this comic strip with her pal Jem and fill in the balloons with your own dialogue.

HOW TO DRAW ROGER

Roger always has a trick up his sleeve, and so does Emily, Beano illustrator! Follow her instructions and have a go!

1

Sketch out a pose using basic shapes. You'll rub these out later. Put a cross on the head to show where he's looking. Roger has one hand behind his back because he's probably hiding something!

2

Draw the outline of Roger's face and add a circle for his nose on the middle line. Draw in the hands, and add in his cuffs and collars.

3

Draw in Roger's hairline, his jumper and trousers.

4

Now it's time to add his fingers. He's got a reassuring thumb pointing towards him as if to say 'I've got this!'. It's also time to draw in his shoes.

5

Add in a confident smile showing his top row of teeth. Draw his eyes touching his nose and don't forget his eyebrows! For the shirt, start by drawing in stripes.

6

To finish his shirt, draw lines going down to make checkers.

7

Draw in Roger's fringe and add the highlight to the back of his head. Now it's time to go over the pencil in pen. Fill in the squares on his shirt, his trousers and hair.

8

Erase your pencil lines underneath the pen (make sure the pen is dry first) and now you're ready to add colours!

ROGER'S POSES AND EXPRESSIONS

Here are some of Roger's best dodges. Practise drawing these poses and add them to your own strips!

Practise drawing Roger and add him to this comic strip. Add your own hilarious dialogue to the balloons.

HOW TO DRAW JEM

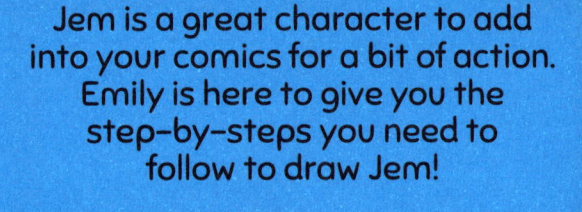

Jem is a great character to add into your comics for a bit of action. Emily is here to give you the step-by-steps you need to follow to draw Jem!

1

Sketch out a pose with basic shapes – keeping in mind that Jem loves to run! Put a cross on the head to show the direction she's looking.

2

Using the rough shapes, draw in the outline of Jem's face, add the shape of her hair and rough out the hand shapes too. Pop her nose on the middle line on her face.

3

Add detail to her hair, and draw in her top, trousers and arms. We'll also draw in her hands at this stage.

4

Add the stripes to her top and draw her running shoes in, so she's not running in bare feet!

5

Draw in her eyes touching her nose and give her a big happy smile – she's at her happiest when she's running! Now would be a good time to draw over your sketch in pen too!

6

Erase your pencil lines underneath the pen (make sure the pen is dry first). Now you're ready to add colours!

EXPERT TIP

JEM IS VERY ACTIVE, THINK ABOUT THIS WHEN DECIDING HER POSE.

JEM'S
POSES AND EXPRESSIONS

Jem is always on the move, so you'll need to practise drawing her in different action poses. Here are some poses to try!

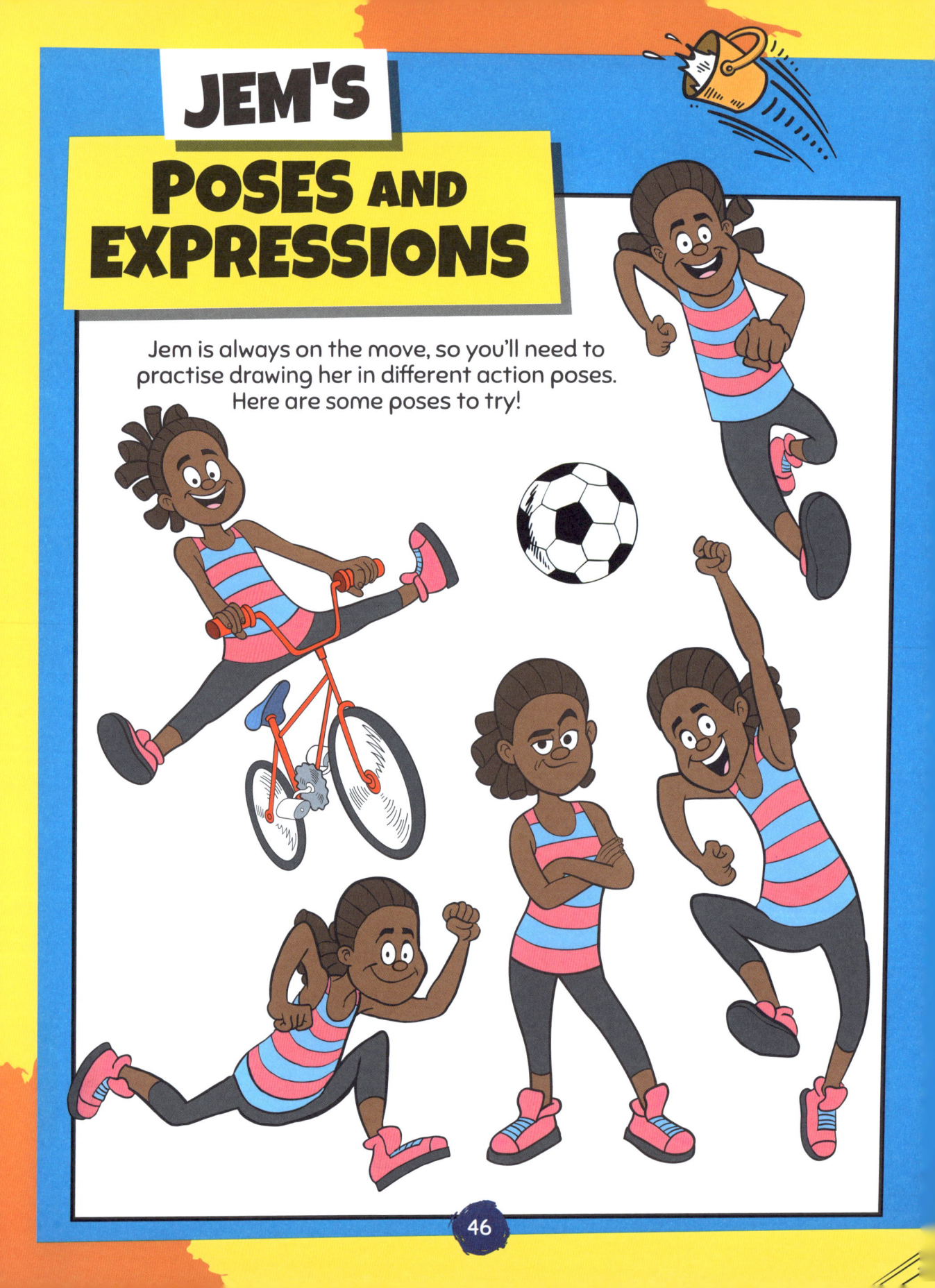

Practise drawing Jem and add her to this comic strip.
Don't forget to add some dialogue!

OTHER CHARACTERS

HEENA

There are plenty of other characters for you to draw in Beanotown. Use the grids to copy them on the following pages!

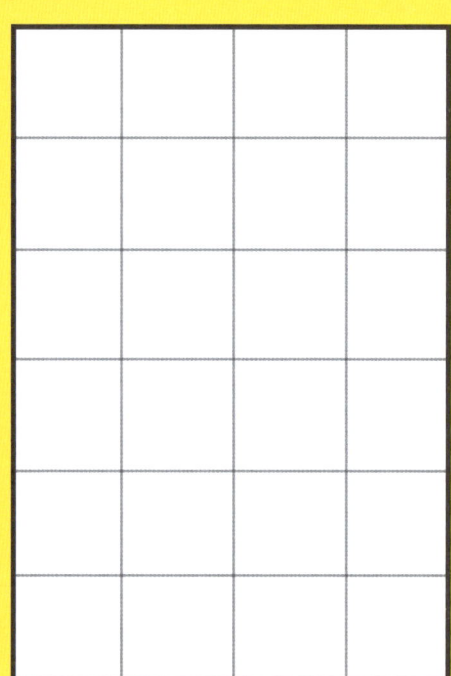

HARI

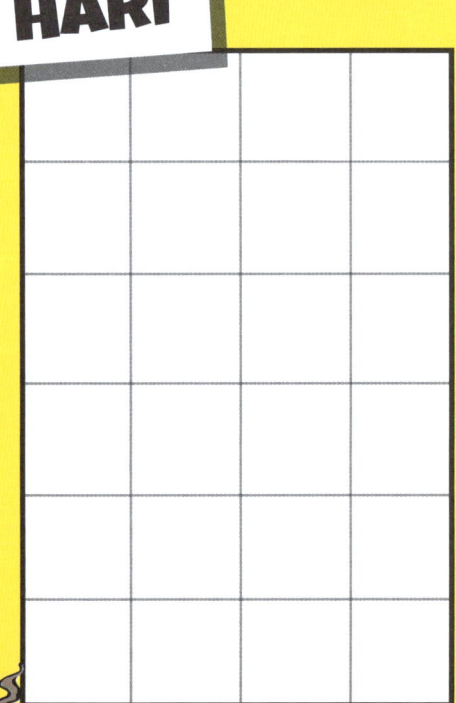

SAHANA

 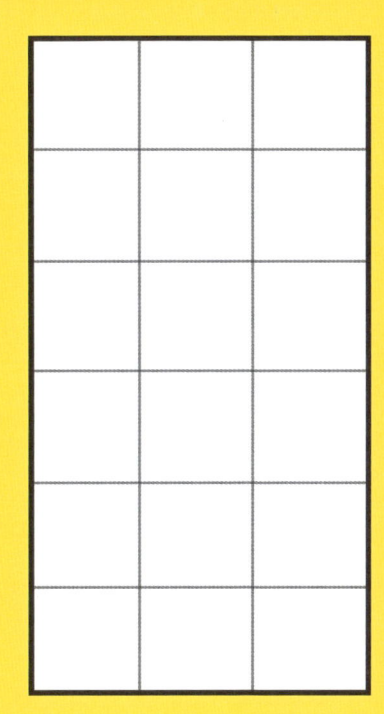 

HANI

 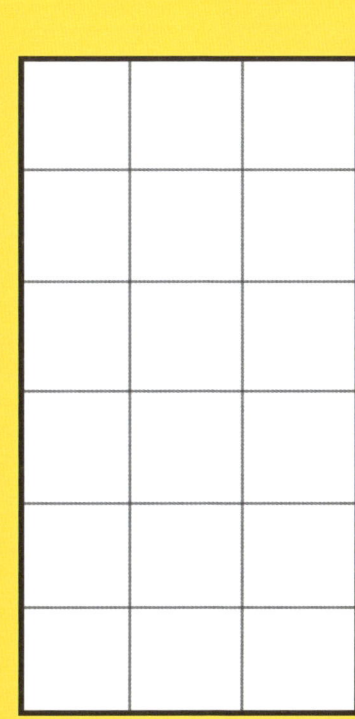 

ERIC WIMP

BANANAMAN

MISS MISTRY

DANGEROUS DAN

SANDRA MENACE

BEA

GRAN MENACE

DENNIS SR

BILLY WHIZZ

ANGEL FACE

RUBI

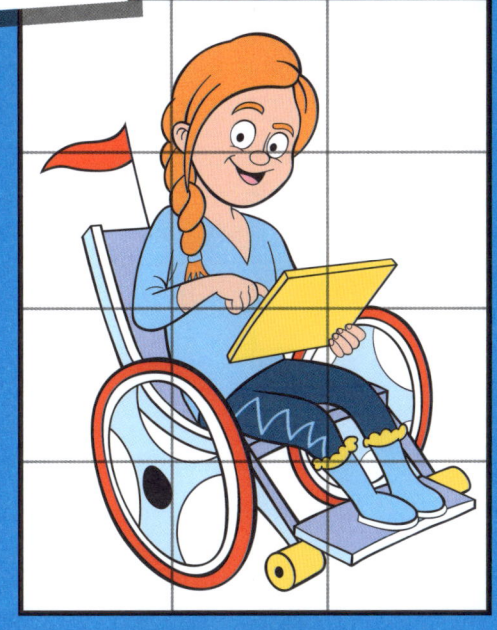

LORD SNOOTY

WALTER

VITO

BERTIE

PIE FACE

THE BASH STREET KIDS

DANNY

GNASHER

WILFRID

MANDI

SIDNEY

SMIFFY

FREDDY

SCOTTY

HARSHA

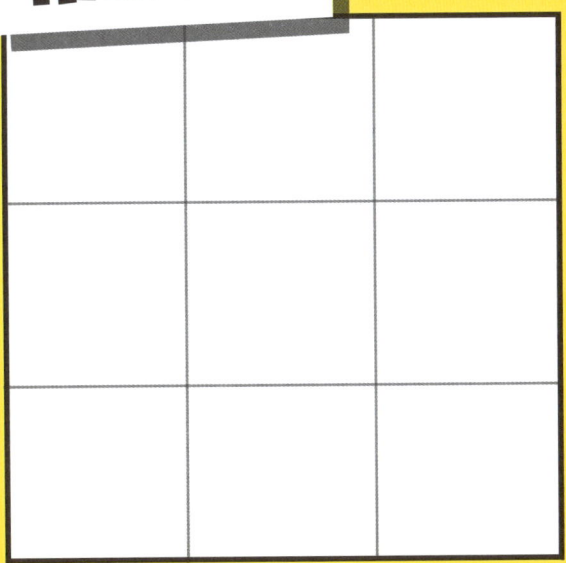

ERBERT

TOOTS

PLUG

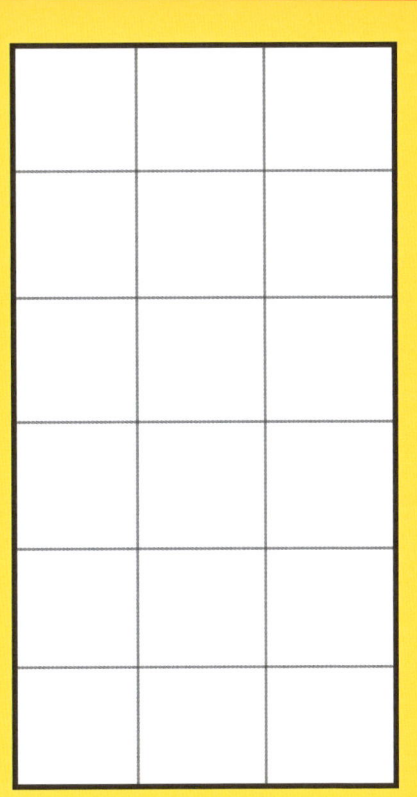

MAHIRA

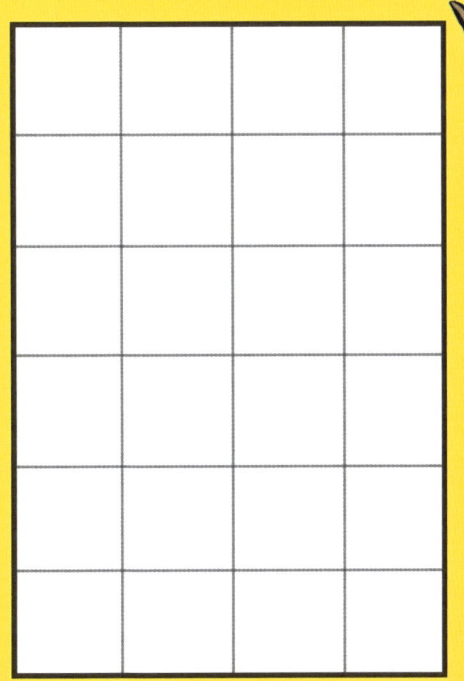

SKETCH KHAD

STEVIE STAR

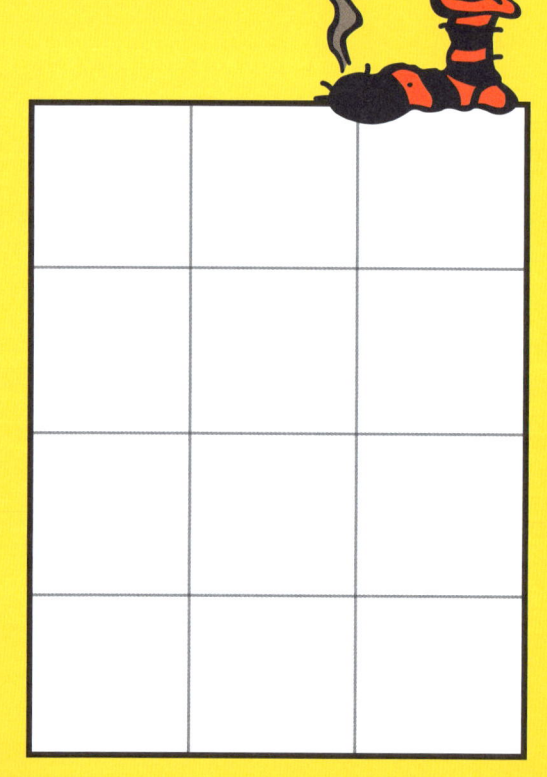

CREATE A CHARACTER

Have you ever wished you could appear in Beano? Here's your chance! Answer this questionnaire to decide what your character will be like, and then turn the page to design them.

BEANO NAME: ....

(TO COME UP WITH YOUR BEANO NAME, THINK OF A WORD THAT STARTS WITH THE SAME LETTER AS YOUR FIRST NAME, BUT ALSO DESCRIBES YOUR CHARACTER OR SPECIAL POWER. FOR EXAMPLE YOU COULD BE JUMPING JAMAL OR MEG THE MAGICIAN!)

AGE: ....

SUPER POWER OR TALENT: ....

CATCHPHRASE: ....

DISTINGUISHING FEATURE: ....

BEST FRIENDS: (TICK THE BOXES BELOW)

☐ ☐ ☐ ☐ ☐ ☐

PET: ....

LIKES: ....

DISLIKES: ....

WANT TO MAKE MORE CHARACTERS? WHY NOT USE THIS QUESTIONNAIRE TO MAKE YOUR FRIENDS AND FAMILY INTO COMIC STARS?

FAVOURITE PLACE IN BEANOTOWN: ....

PROUDEST MOMENT: ....

....

MOST EMBARRASSING MOMENT: ....

....

FAVOURITE PRANKING DEVICE: (TICK THE BOXES BELOW)

FAVOURITE OUTFIT: ....

DESIGN YOUR CHARACTER

Now you know almost everything about your new star character, it's time to bring them to life. Draw a body outline below, and then sketch some details.

COMIC CHARACTERS ARE EXAGGERATED, SO WHY NOT GIVE YOUR CHARACTER A BIG HAIRSTYLE?

THINK ABOUT HOW YOUR CHARACTER IS FEELING, AND SHOW THIS ON THEIR FACE.

IS YOUR CHARACTER HOLDING ANYTHING? PERHAPS THEY'VE GOT A PRANKING DEVICE READY!

DRESS YOUR CHARACTER IN THEIR FAVOURITE OUTFIT. IT'S A GOOD IDEA TO PICK A SIMPLE DESIGN, AS YOU DON'T WANT TO HAVE TO REDRAW SOMETHING COMPLICATED EIGHT TIMES ON A PAGE!

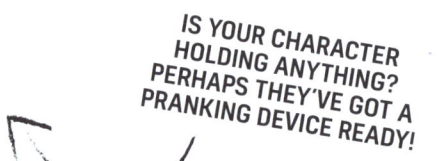

EXPERT TIP

IF YOU WANT TO DRAW A POSE, ASK A FRIEND TO STRIKE IT, AND THEN MAKE A QUICK SKETCH OF THE SHAPE THEIR BODY MAKES.

Fill in these faces to reflect the different emotions the character is feeling.

ANGRY

SILLY

HAPPY

MISCHIEVOUS

BORED

LAUGHING

USING THE PENCIL, INK AND COLOUR METHOD, DRAW YOUR CHARACTER IN FULL.

MISCHIEF COMIC STRIP

It's time for your character to make their Beano debut – add them into the scenes below and write some dialogue to complete the story.

CREATE A COMIC

PHUT!

So you've got a story to tell and you've learned how to draw the characters you're going to include in it. Congrats! You're now ready to learn how to create yourself a comic!

There's a lot to consider when drawing a comic. Not only do you need to know how to draw your characters in various poses, but you'll need to be able to draw them in scenes, interacting with other characters and props.

Sounds complicated, huh? Don't worry – in this chapter, we'll be taking you through everything you need to learn to be able to create a brilliant comic book!

HOW TO DRAW PROPS

You're now pretty good at drawing comic book characters (unless you skipped the last chapter!) so it's time to practise drawing props! Props are objects that characters use, such as skateboards to whizz them around and squishy tomatoes that they use in pranks.

Here are some Beano-riffic props for you to use in your comic strips. Try copying them in the boxes below.

EXPERT TIP

IF YOU'RE HAVING TROUBLE COPYING SOMETHING, TRACE A 3 X 3 GRID OVER THE TOP OF IT, AND THEN COPY THE PICTURE, SQUARE BY SQUARE, INTO AN EMPTY GRID. TRY IT HERE!

 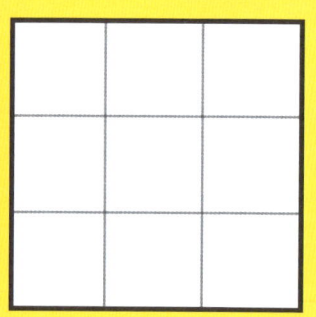

 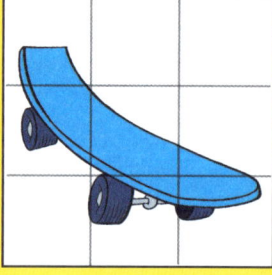  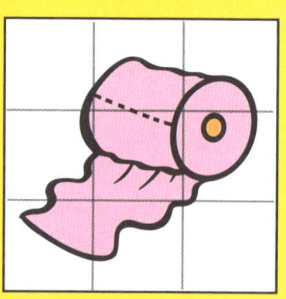

  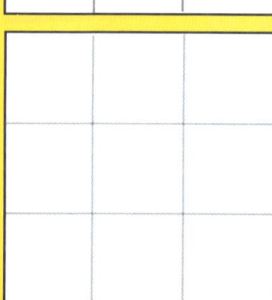

EXPERT TIP

DO YOU WANT TO ADD A PROP THAT'S NOT IN THIS BOOK? FIND THE OBJECT (OR A PICTURE OF IT) TO COPY AND DRAW IT IN PENCIL FIRST. IF IT'S COMPLICATED, TRY BREAKING IT DOWN INTO SHAPES FIRST, AND THEN ADD THE DETAIL.

DESIGN A
SUPER-FAST SCOOTER

CREATE A BRAND-NEW
PRANKING DEVICE

DRAW A SANDWICH
FIT FOR A MENACE

ADDING PROPS TO COMIC STRIPS

Use props from the last two pages, or your own designs, to bring these comic strips to life! Don't forget to add some words too!

HOW TO DRAW BACKGROUNDS

You can't have all the amazing characters, action and props on a white backdrop (unless your story takes place in a white void of nothingness), so you'll need to add backgrounds.

A background is used to set the scene. It helps the reader work out where the story is taking place (is it inside, outside, on the moon, underground?) and when the action is happening (is it night, day, winter, summer?).

Sometimes the background will show a specific location (such as Bash Street School or Dennis's house) and sometimes it will just show a generic scene (trees and a blue sky instantly tell the reader the character is outside on a sunny day!).

The background you use will depend on a few things:

WHERE the story is taking place (obviously!)

THE SIZE of the panel you are drawing in (you can show more in a wide panel)

THE VIEW OF THE ACTION – is it a close-up on the character's face, or is it a wider shot showing more of their body and more background?

EXPERT TIP

IF YOU ARE CREATING YOUR OWN COMIC BOOK WORLD, YOU COULD PUT TOGETHER A MOOD BOARD OF REAL-LIFE BUILDINGS AND LOCATIONS THAT INSPIRE YOU.

Here are some Beano backgrounds for you to use and copy.

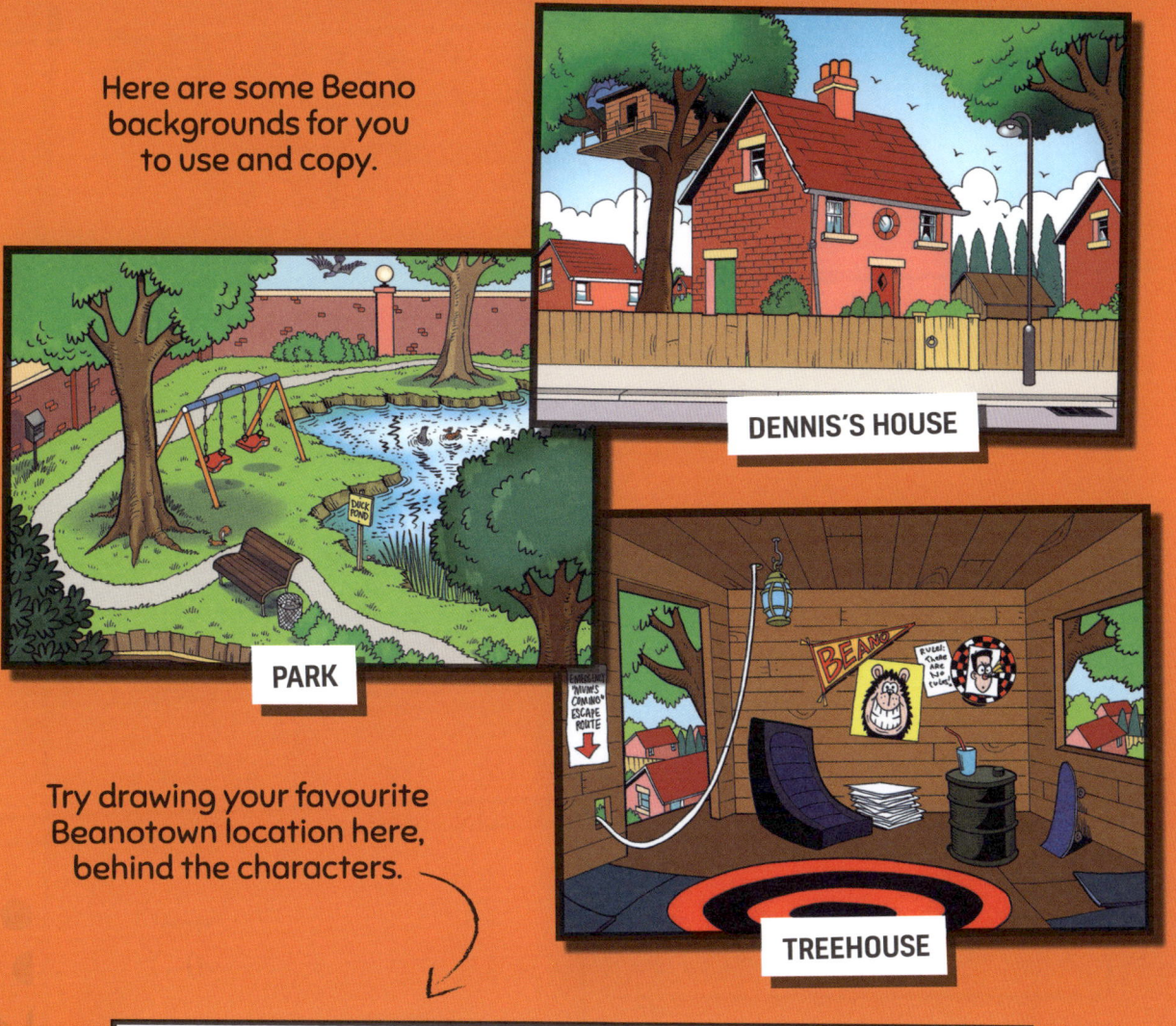

DENNIS'S HOUSE

PARK

TREEHOUSE

Try drawing your favourite Beanotown location here, behind the characters.

ADDING BACKGROUNDS TO COMIC STRIPS

Decide where the action in these comic strips is taking place, and add the background details. Remember to decide if the panel is showing a close–up or zoomed–out scene. When you're done, add some funny dialogue.

HOW TO DRAW
SOUND EFFECTS

You might think that sound effects (or SFX) are reserved for blockbuster movies and TV dramas, but you can totally have sound in your comics. They're not sounds you can hear, but you can make the reader imagine what the comic sounds like, just by using a word, an interesting shape, a cool font and bright colours. Sound effects can add humour, build tension and even provide action. You can add SFX to your comic strips, either within panels – or even taking up a whole panel (if it's a really, really, really, REALLY loud noise).

SHAPE – Think about the shape you want to put your sound effect in. Is the noise jagged and sharp, soft and fluffy or gloopy and runny? By placing the SFX into a shape (or burst), you can give the reader an idea of what sound they should imagine.

FONT – The font type and size can really help the reader to 'hear' the sound. Should the word be in capitals, or all lower case? Should the letters be crowded together, or spaced out? Try whispering, saying or shouting the noise, and imagine what it could look like written down.

WORD – The word you choose for your sound effect should be onomatopoeic (that means it sounds like the sound). There are some amazing onomatopoeic words that already exist like

BOOM! FIZZLE Splat! roar! and CRUNCH!

POP!

If a word doesn't exist for the sound, you can make one up. Simply listen to the sound, or try to make it yourself, and think about which letters you could use to make the noise.

Copy these SFX and use them in your comic strips:

Try creating your own SFX bursts for these noises.
You might have to invent a new word:

HEAVY RAIN

THE LOUDEST
BURP EVER

ESCAPING GAS

A SPOOKY GHOST

AN ANGRY SEAGULL

ADDING SOUND EFFECTS TO COMIC STRIPS

Look at what's happening in these comic strips, and add your own SFX bursts and balloons to help the reader 'hear' all the noises! Finish off by adding in some dialogue.

GNASH! GNASH!

CAPTIONS AND BALLOONS

It is true; a picture speaks a thousand words, but ACTUAL words are useful to help move the plot along. In comics, you can include text in caption boxes, in dialogue (speech balloons) and in thought bubbles.

ADD DRAWINGS TO THE COMIC STRIP BELOW TO SEE HOW THE CAPTION BOXES WORK.

A CAPTION BOX IS THAT LITTLE BOX AT THE TOP (OR SOMETIMES BOTTOM) OF A PANEL. IT DOESN'T INCLUDE DIALOGUE, BUT IS INSTEAD THE VOICE OF THE AUTHOR – AND SOMETIMES EDITOR. IT'S USED TO SET THE SCENE AT THE BEGINNING OF A STRIP OR TO EXPLAIN THE STORY IN MORE DETAIL. IT'S ALSO USED TO SHOW A CHANGE IN TIME OR LOCATION.

CAPTION BOXES

THE STORY IS SET UP HERE.

THIS CAPTION TELLS US THAT TIME HAS MOVED ON.

MINNIE HAS WOKEN UP, FEELING MISCHIEVOUS . . .

TEE-HEE-HEE! I HAVE A PLAN!

LATER THAT DAY . . .

OUCH THAT LOOKS LIKE IT HURTS! – THE ED

SOMETIMES THE EDITOR ADDS A FUNNY COMMENT IN A CAPTION BOX.

SPEECH BALLOONS

A lot of the story in a comic strip is shown through what the characters say – in other words, the dialogue. This is shown through speech balloons.

WHEN YOU WRITE SPEECH, TRY TO MAKE IT SOUND NATURAL – AND THINK ABOUT WHETHER THE CHARACTER SPEAKS IN A CERTAIN WAY. YOU COULD TEST THIS OUT BY SPEAKING THE LINES OUT LOUD, IN THAT CHARACTER'S VOICE.

IF YOUR CHARACTER HAS A LOT TO SAY,

YOU CAN SPLIT THE BALLOONS LIKE THIS.

LIKE SFX, YOU CAN SHOW IF SOMEONE IS SHOUTING BY USING A SPIKY BURST . . .

. . . OR SHOW SOMEONE IS WHISPERING WITH A DOTTED BALLOON.

THIS IS A STANDARD SPEECH BALLOON, THE TAIL SHOULD POINT TOWARDS THE CHARACTER'S MOUTH.

THOUGHT BUBBLES

Characters don't always speak their minds; sometimes they can let the readers know their secrets through thought bubbles!

Write or draw in what these characters are thinking about:

THOUGHT BUBBLES CAN BE USED TO:

· SHOW WHAT CHARACTERS WHO DON'T SPEAK (SUCH AS ANIMALS) ARE THINKING

· SHOW WHAT A CHARACTER REALLY THINKS (THIS IS OFTEN DIFFERENT TO WHAT THEY'RE SAYING)

· SHOW WHAT A CHARACTER IS DREAMING ABOUT – USUALLY A DREAM BUBBLE WILL CONTAIN PICTURES RATHER THAN WORDS

· TELL A CHARACTER'S SECRET PLAN

ADDING CAPTIONS AND BALLOONS TO

COMIC STRIPS

Complete this comic strip, adding in caption boxes, speech balloons, thought bubbles and – of course – the words to go with them!

PLANNING A
COMIC STRIP

You're nearly ready to draw your own comic strip, but first, it's a good idea to create a plan of what will happen in each panel. This will help you work out what size each panel needs to be, how big to draw your speech balloons and if there are any gaps in your story. Have a look at this example, and then turn the page to plan your own strip!

Panel 1:   Dennis wakes up. 'Ugh, I can't believe I have to go to school today.'

Panel 2:   Sleepy Dennis goes downstairs to have breakfast. Mum and Dad aren't there.

Panel 3:   Dennis on skateboard going to school. Postman: 'You're up early, Dennis!'

Panel 4:   Dennis decides to play a trick on Walter, so hides in a bush on Walter's route.

Panel 5:   10 minutes later . . . 'I guess Walter's off sick today.' Gnasher shrugs.

Panel 6:   Dennis approaches the school.

Panel 7:   Close-up on Dennis trying to open the door. 'Hmm, it's locked!'

Panel 8:   Dennis's mum pulls up in the car. 'DENNIS! What are you doing? It's Saturday!'

Panel 9:   Dennis facepalms!

PLANNING A
COMIC STRIP

Now it's your turn! Start by writing down all the scenes you need to show, and then roughly sketch them out on the next page.

Panel 1: --

Panel 2: --

Panel 3: --

Panel 4: --

Panel 5: --

Panel 6: --

Panel 7: --

Panel 8: --

Panel 9: --

CREATE YOUR OWN

COMIC STRIPS

You're finally ready. Fill these pages with your own comic strips!

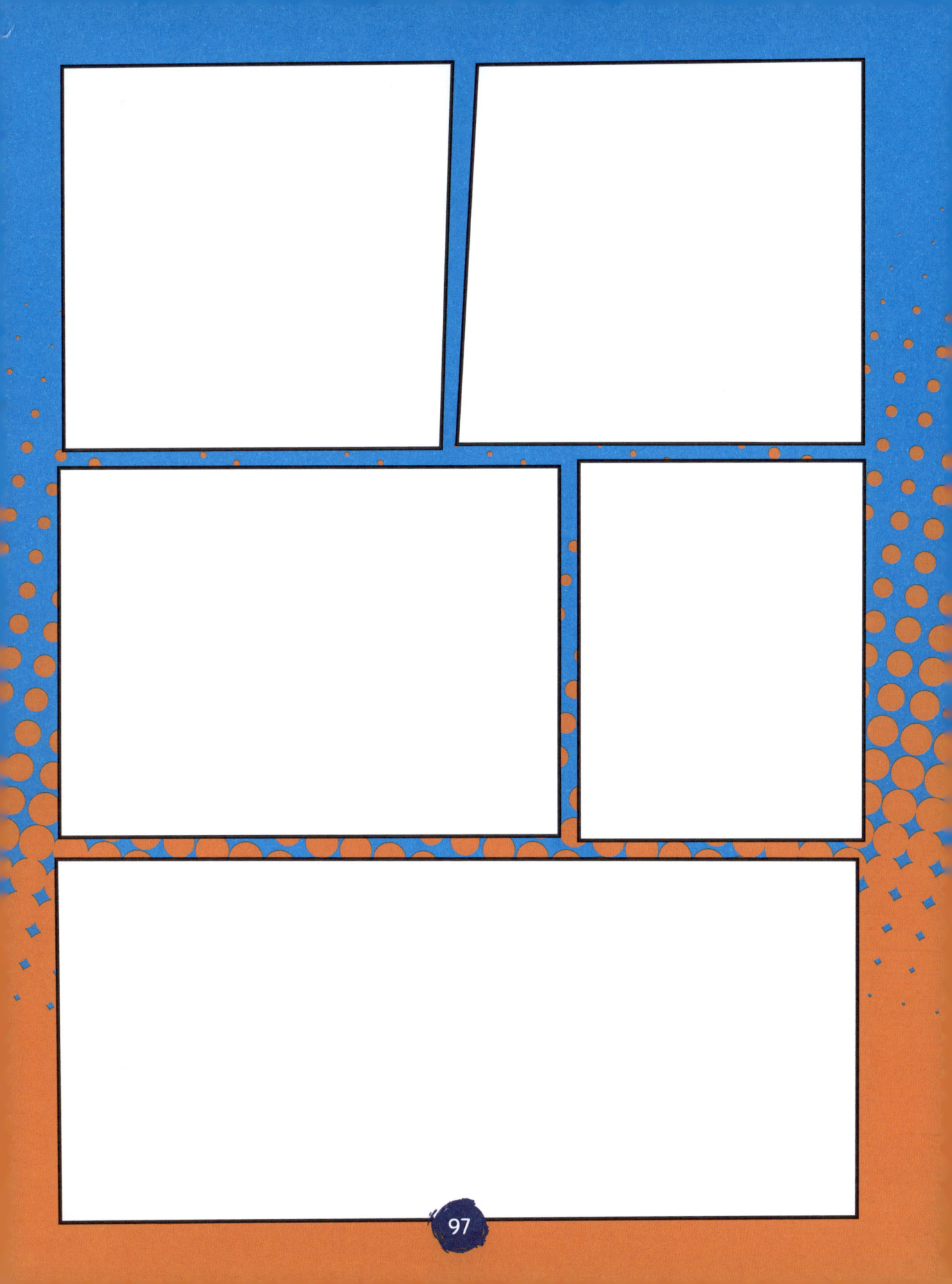

CREATING A COVER

You may have heard people say 'don't judge a book by its cover', but the truth is, we all do. Look at the cover for this book. It's awesome, right? It makes you want to open it up and start creating your own comic. You want the cover of your comic to grab the reader's attention, and to give them a teaser of what's inside. Just take a look at your favourite Beano covers for inspiration.

THIS COULD BE SOMETHING SEASONAL OR SOMETHING INCLUDED IN THE COMIC, SUCH AS A FEATURE OR COMPETITION!

ADD A SUPER-FUN CAPTION HERE!

BEANO

INTERESTING AND EPIC COMIC TITLE

YOU COULD ADD THE TITLE OF THE MOST EXCITING STRIP HERE OR ADD A PHRASE THAT SUMS UP THE THEME OF THE COMIC. USE BRIGHT, BOLD LETTERING THAT STANDS OUT.

PLUS!	PLUS!	PLUS!
What else is in your comic? Are there more stories?	Are there puzzles, games or pranks?	Who else features in your comic strips?

YOU CAN ADD IN EXTRA BOXES OR PANELS THAT SHOW WHAT ELSE IS INCLUDED IN THE COMIC BOOK.

 PHUT!

 PEAS

HAVE A GO AT COMPLETING YOUR OWN BEANO COVER ON ON THE NEXT FEW PAGES!

BEANO

BEANO

BEANO

MAKE YOUR OWN

That's it! We've taught you everything you need to know to be able to create your very own Beano comic book. All that's left is for you to go ahead and make one yourself!

This chapter is full of space for you to craft and draw your own stories – unless, of course, this book belongs to a friend or library! It's not nice to draw in other people's books, is it? But that doesn't mean you should miss out – grab yourself some paper and trace any sections you wish to copy. Same goes for when you inevitably run out of space for all your incredible ideas!

BEANO®

TITLE

BEGINNING

WHO IS THE MAIN CHARACTER OF THE STORY? --

WHAT DOES THE CHARACTER WANT OR NEED? --

WHERE IS THE STORY SET? --

MIDDLE

WHAT PROBLEM DOES YOUR CHARACTER COME UP AGAINST? ---------------------------------

----

HOW DOES YOUR CHARACTER REACT TO THE PROBLEM? ------------------------------------

----

HOW DOES THE CHARACTER FEEL? ---

WHAT'S THE MAIN ACTION? ---

END

HOW IS THE PROBLEM SOLVED? --

HOW DOES YOUR CHARACTER FEEL? ---

THIS STORYLINE IS AWESOME!

BLANK COMIC STRIP PLOTTING SHEETS

Use the blank plotting sheets to plan your comic strips. Remember to write down what you want to happen in each panel and then roughly sketch the action.

Panel 1: --

Panel 2: --

Panel 3: --

Panel 4: --

Panel 5: --

Panel 6: --

Panel 7: --

Panel 8: --

Panel 9: --

WHAT HAPPENS NEXT?

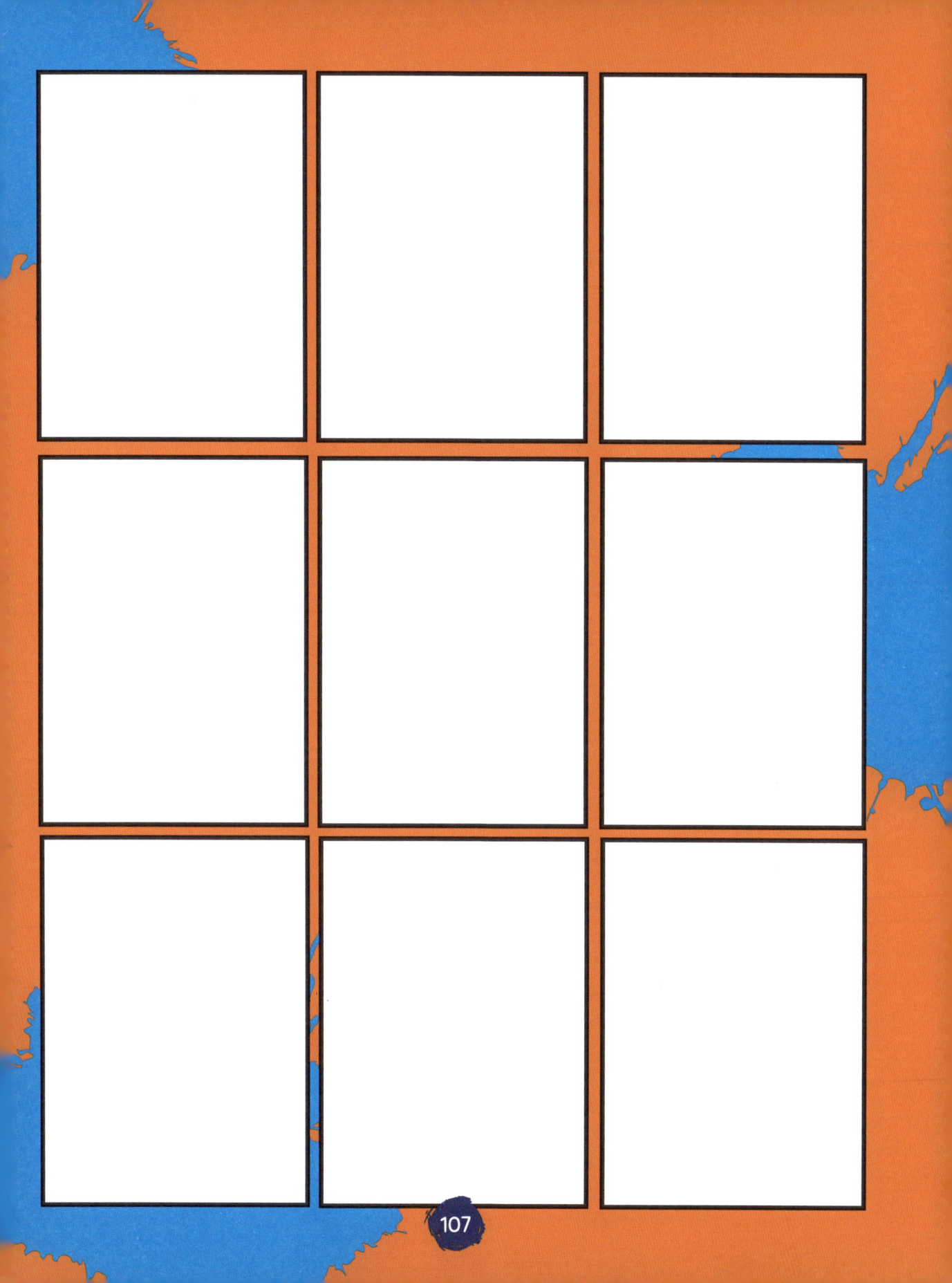

CREATE YOUR OWN

COMIC STRIPS

Draw your final comic strip here!

BEANO

TITLE

BEGINNING

WHO IS THE MAIN CHARACTER OF THE STORY?--------------------------------

WHAT DOES THE CHARACTER WANT OR NEED? ----------------------------------

----

WHERE IS THE STORY SET? ---

MIDDLE

WHAT PROBLEM DOES YOUR CHARACTER COME UP AGAINST? ---------------------

----

HOW DOES YOUR CHARACTER REACT TO THE PROBLEM? -------------------------

----

HOW DOES THE CHARACTER FEEL? ---

WHAT'S THE MAIN ACTION? --

END

HOW IS THE PROBLEM SOLVED? ---

HOW DOES YOUR CHARACTER FEEL? --

MAKE ME A SUPERHERO!

Plotting sheet

Panel 1: ....
....

Panel 2: ....
....

Panel 3: ....
....

Panel 4: ....
....

Panel 5: ....
....

Panel 6: ....
....

Panel 7: ....
....

Panel 8: ....
....

Panel 9: ....
....

WRITE ME INTO YOUR STORY!

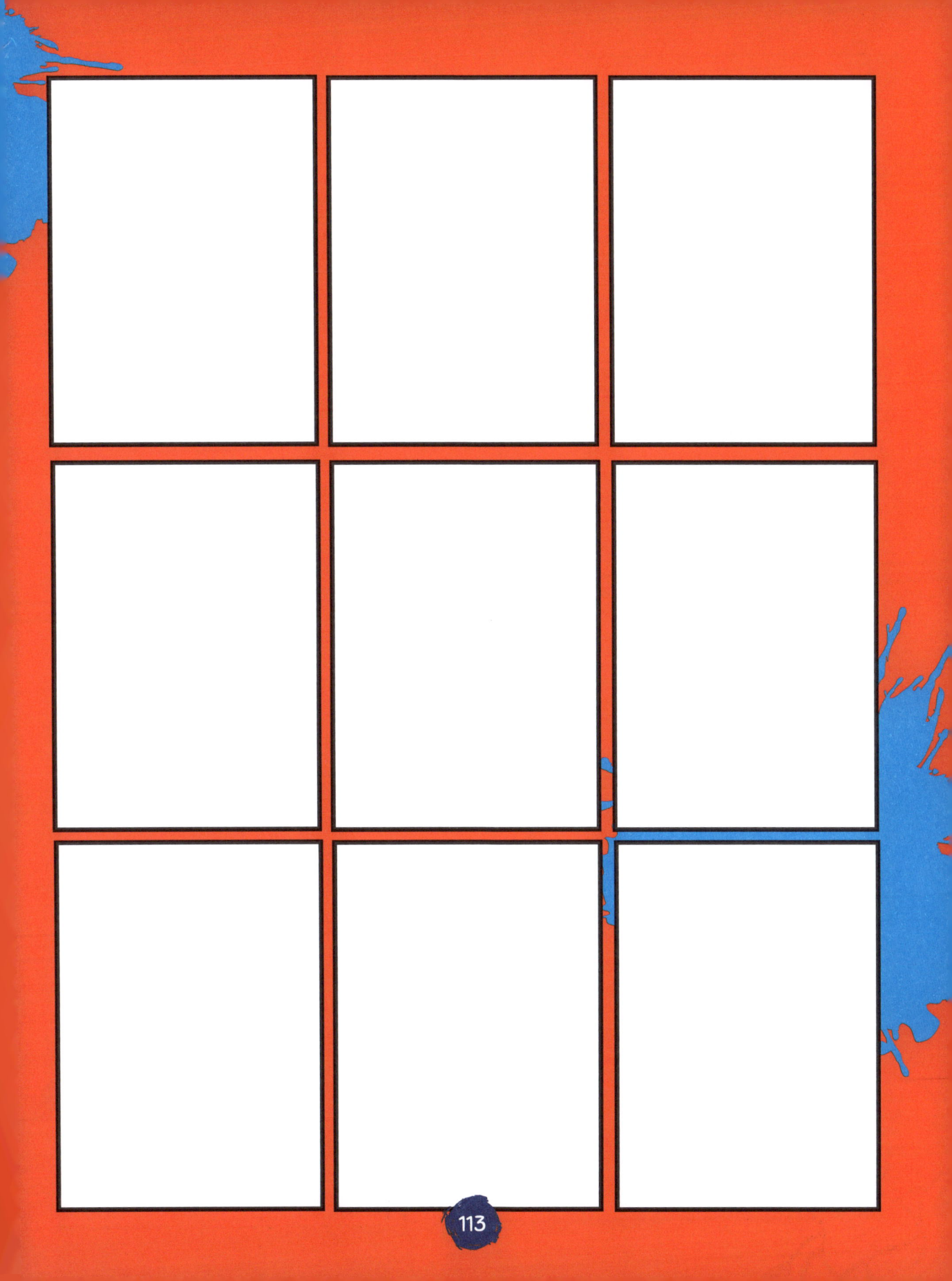

IT'S TIME FOR ERIC TO EAT A BANANA!

114

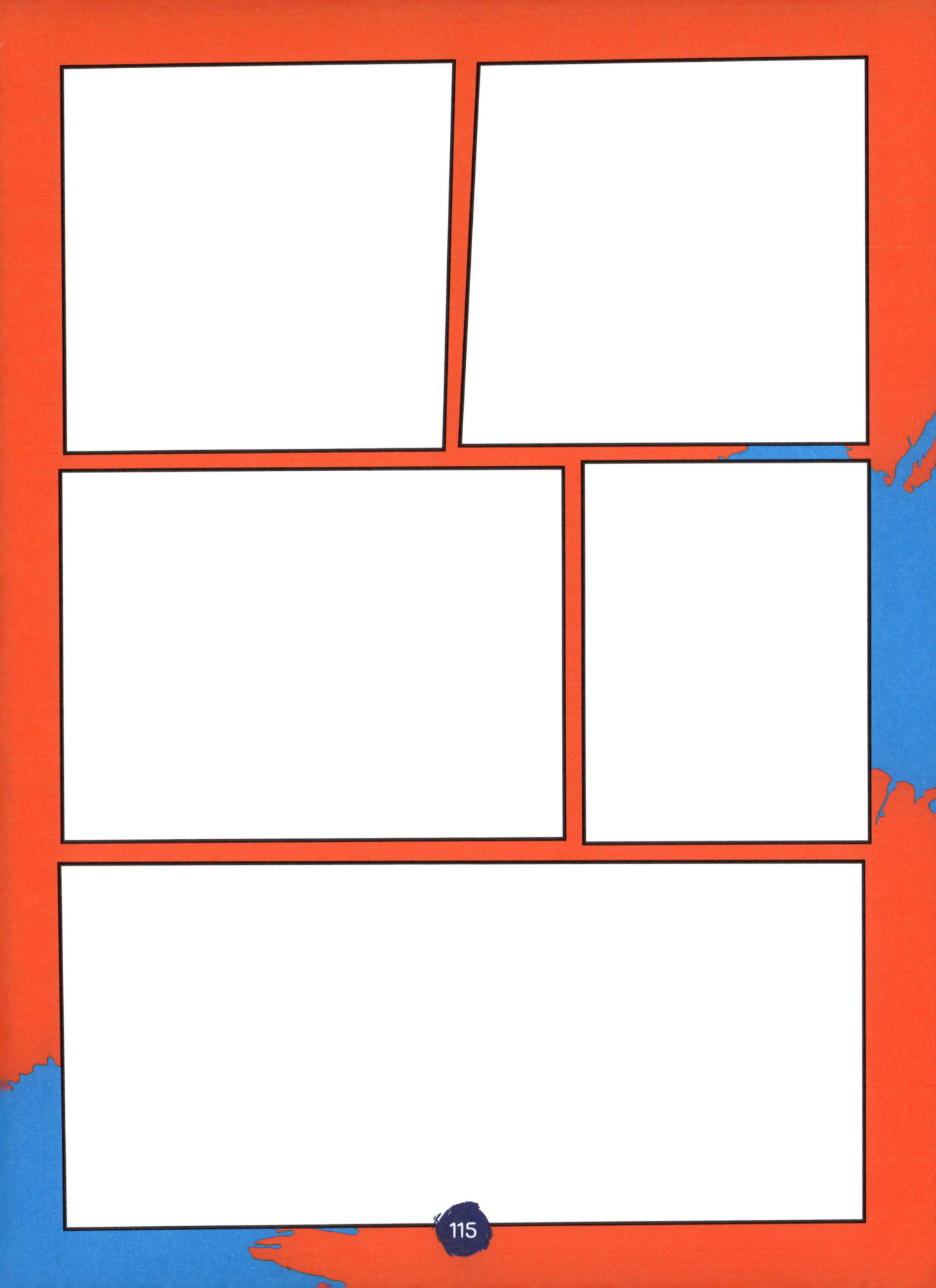

BEANO

TITLE

BEGINNING

WHO IS THE MAIN CHARACTER OF THE STORY? ----------

WHAT DOES THE CHARACTER WANT OR NEED? ----------

WHERE IS THE STORY SET? ----------

MIDDLE

WHAT PROBLEM DOES YOUR CHARACTER COME UP AGAINST? ----------

HOW DOES YOUR CHARACTER REACT TO THE PROBLEM? ----------

HOW DOES THE CHARACTER FEEL? ----------

WHAT'S THE MAIN ACTION? ----------

END

HOW IS THE PROBLEM SOLVED? ----------

HOW DOES YOUR CHARACTER FEEL? ----------

GNASH GNASH GNICE STORY!

Plotting sheet

Panel 1: --

Panel 2: --

Panel 3: --

Panel 4: --

Panel 5: --

Panel 6: --

Panel 7: --

Panel 8: --

Panel 9: --

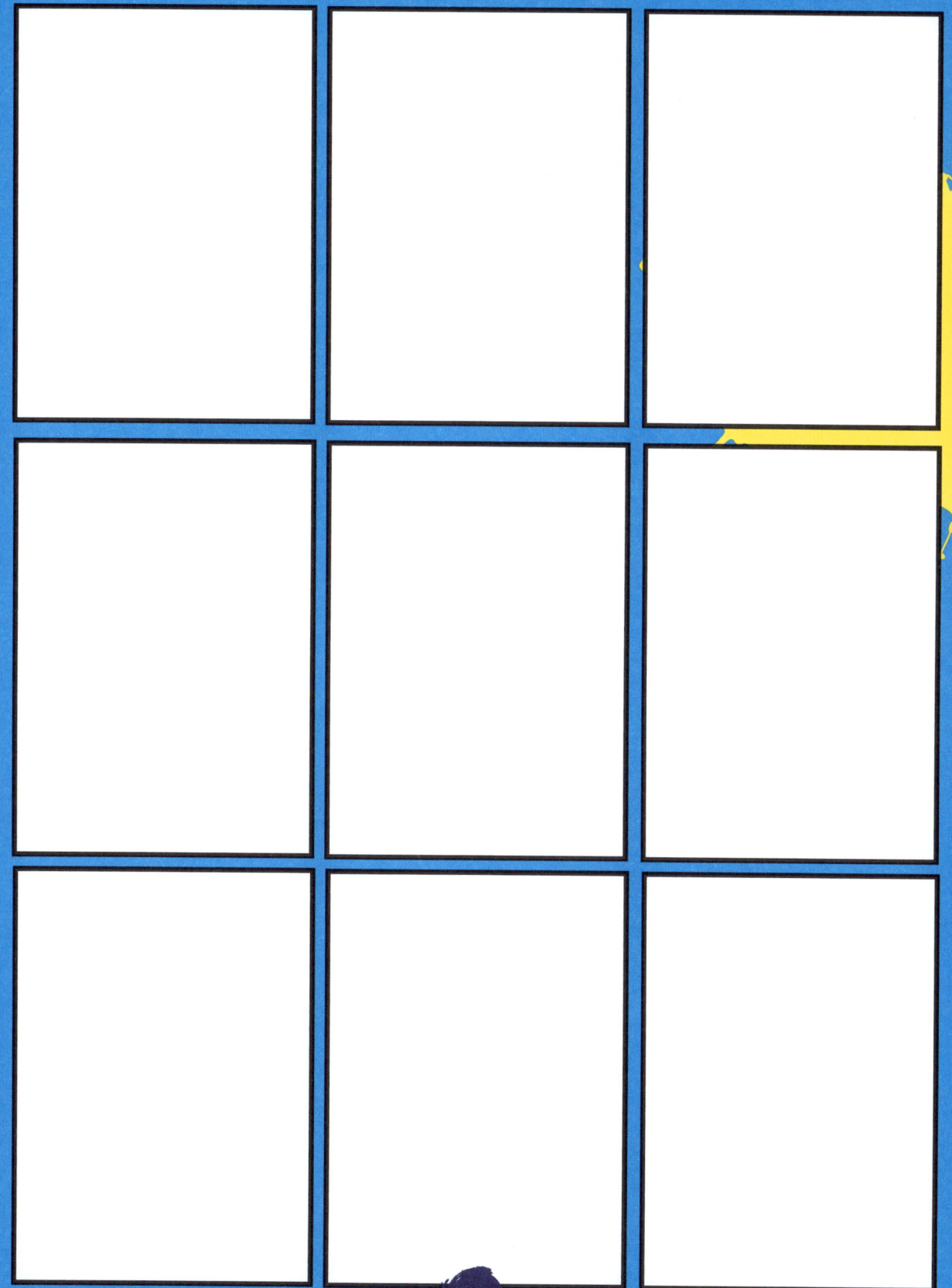

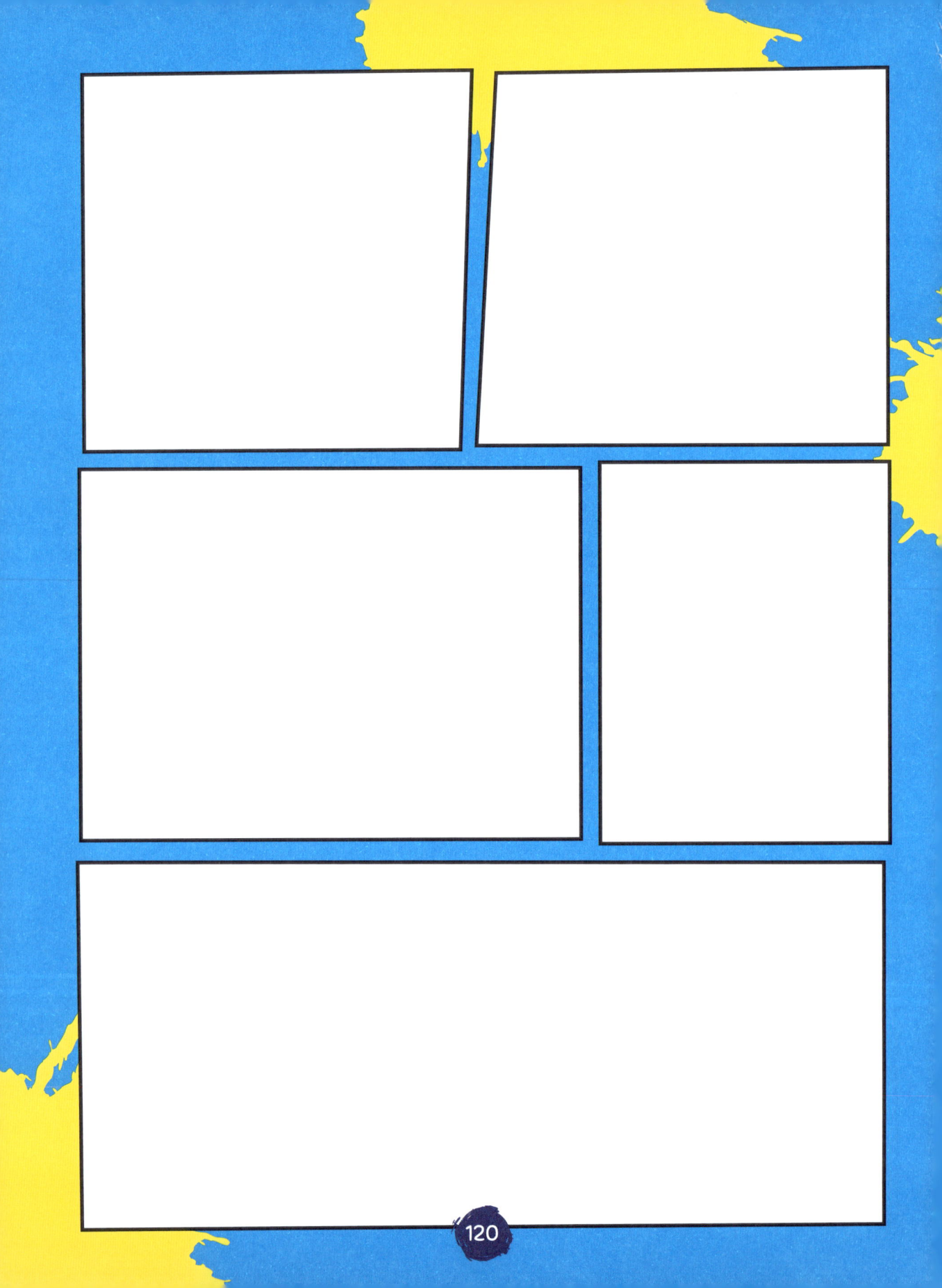

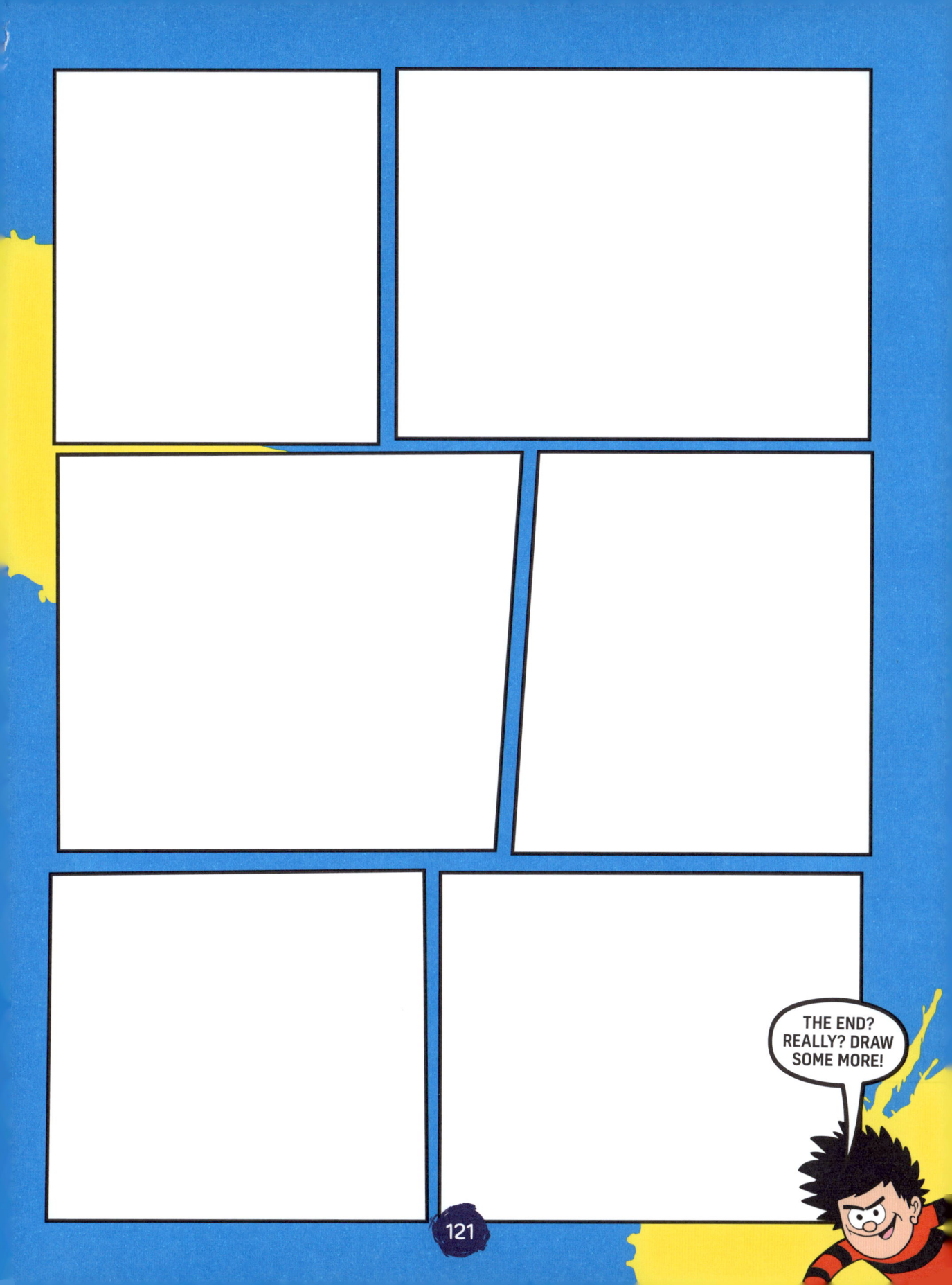

THE END?
REALLY? DRAW
SOME MORE!

BEANO

TITLE

_____

BEGINNING

WHO IS THE MAIN CHARACTER OF THE STORY?_____

WHAT DOES THE CHARACTER WANT OR NEED? _____

_____

WHERE IS THE STORY SET? _____

_____

MIDDLE

WHAT PROBLEM DOES YOUR CHARACTER COME UP AGAINST? _____

_____

_____

HOW DOES YOUR CHARACTER REACT TO THE PROBLEM? _____

_____

HOW DOES THE CHARACTER FEEL? _____

_____

WHAT'S THE MAIN ACTION? _____

_____

END

HOW IS THE PROBLEM SOLVED? _____

_____

_____

HOW DOES YOUR CHARACTER FEEL? _____

_____

_____

WHAT IF ALIENS INVADED?!

Plotting sheet

Panel 1: ....

Panel 2: ....

Panel 3: ....

Panel 4: ....

Panel 5: ....

Panel 6: ....

Panel 7: ....

Panel 8: ....

Panel 9: ....

I SHOULD BE IN THIS ONE!